NICOLAE HIGH

Tyndale House books by Tim LaHaye and Jerry B. Jenkins

The Left Behind series
Left Behind
Tribulation Force
Nicolae
Soul Harvest
Apollyon
Assassins
Book 7 available spring 2000

Left Behind: The Kids
#1: The Vanishings
#2: Second Chance
#3: Through the Flames
#4: Facing the Future
#5: Nicolae High
#6: The Underground Paper

Tyndale House books by Tim LaHaye
How to Be Happy though Married
Spirit-Controlled Temperament
Transformed Temperaments
Why You Act the Way You Do

Tyndale House books by Jerry Jenkins
And Then Came You
As You Leave Home
Still the One

Nicolae High

5

LEFT BEHIND™

>THE KIDS<

Jerry B. Jenkins

Tim LaHaye

TYNDALE KIDS

TYNDALE HOUSE PUBLISHERS, INC.
WHEATON, ILLINOIS

Visit Tyndale's exciting Web site at www.tyndale.com

Discover the latest Left Behind news at www.leftbehind.com

Left Behind is a trademark of Tyndale House Publishers.

Published in association with the literary agency of Alive Communications, Inc., 1465 Kelly Johnson Blvd., Suite 320, Colorado Springs, CO 80920.

Edited by Rick Blanchette
Designed by Jenny Destree

ISBN 0-8423-4325-3

Printed in the United States of America

05 04 03 02 01 00 99
9   8   7   6   5   4   3   2   1

To Michael B. Jenkins

CONTENTS

What's Gone On Before

JUDD Thompson Jr. and the other three kids living in his house were involved in the adventure of a lifetime. They had been left alone when their families disappeared in the global vanishings.

Judd was the oldest at sixteen. His father, mother, and younger brother and sister disappeared.

Vicki Byrne, fourteen, lost her parents and her little sister, who all vanished. Her brother in Michigan also disappeared.

Lionel Washington, thirteen, lost his parents, an older sister, and two younger siblings—all vanished.

Ryan Daley, twelve, lost his parents in accidents related to the disappearances.

The four kids had stumbled onto each other and a young pastor, Bruce Barnes, at New Hope Village Church in their town, Mount Prospect, Illinois. Bruce taught that the vanishings had been foretold in the Bible and that the worldwide event was the rapture of the church of Jesus Christ. True believers had been taken to heaven.

Ryan was the last of the four to make the decision to believe in Christ, to trust Jesus for forgiveness of sin, and to assure himself that he would go to be with God when he died.

While dealing with their grief and fear over the loss of their families, the four strived to learn as much as they could about what had happened and what was to come.

Bruce taught that the Rapture was not the beginning of the seven-year tribulation, where the earth and its people would suffer. Rather, he said, the Bible indicated that a great leader would arise, the Antichrist, the great enemy of God. He would make a pact with Israel, and the day that was signed would signal the beginning of the seven years.

Judd, for one, was proud to be a part of this little group, in this church, under this pastor. Judd and his friends were just kids to some people, but they called themselves the Young Tribulation Force. Their task was clear. Their goal was nothing less than to stand against and fight the enemies of God during the seven most chaotic years the planet would ever see.

ONE

Danger on the Road

Judd was stunned. Vicki was gone.

"Where is she?" he demanded.

Lionel and Ryan looked up from their spots on the floor before the TV. Ryan shrugged. "There's a note by the phone."

Judd grabbed it and read quickly. "Hitching to Michigan to see Bub. Back soon."

He slapped the note on his thigh and caught himself before he swore. What was he so mad about? This was his fault.

Vicki had asked him to drive her to see her big brother Eddie's buddy. Judd refused before he thought about it, telling her he felt responsible for Lionel and Ryan and had better stay with them.

"Let them ride along," Vicki had said.

"Nah," Judd said. "The roads are just starting to reopen. We don't really know where we're going. There are rumors school is going

1

to open again, and I'd hate to be out of state if that happens."

"You're going back to school?"

"If it opens, sure."

"Why?"

"Because we have to."

"We have to? Judd, what are they going to do if we don't show up? They'll figure we disappeared along with thousands of others. Anyway, if Bruce is right and there's a peace treaty signed between the UN and Israel, we'll have only seven years left to live. Why would I want to spend half that time in school? To learn what? The world is going to hell, and we'd be sitting in class, trying to prepare for a future that doesn't exist."

She had a point. Judd was a junior, but Vicki was a freshman. School did seem like a waste of time, but Judd didn't know what he thought about breaking the law by refusing to go. If it came to that, he assumed they would all go, Lionel and Ryan back to Lincoln Junior High, he and Vicki to Prospect High.

Judd had underestimated how desperate Vicki was to locate Bub. She had never met him, had only seen pictures and talked to him on the phone—the last time the morning of the Rapture. Her brother had met him when he ran off to work in Michigan after high school. Eddie said he liked Bub at first because he was a wild party kind of a guy. But then Eddie became a Christian. He wasn't able to persuade Bub to quit his loose living, but he kept rooming with him anyway. It was Bub who had confirmed to Vicki that Eddie had disappeared in the Rapture.

"I've been having trouble reaching Bub by phone," she had told Judd. "I want to just go find him."

Judd thought it was a bad idea and said so. He even thought about telling Bruce, but the kids had agreed they weren't going to treat Bruce like a parent. If Judd had known Vicki was going to just leave and hitchhike to Michigan, he would have taken her himself. He hated to think of her out there alone on the road. He felt responsible for her, though he knew he really wasn't. The four of them were on their own now. They all lived together in Judd's house, sure, but it had been their choice to accept his invitation. The only rules were that they would always tell each other where they were. Vicki had fulfilled that requirement.

Judd missed Vicki. There was no other way to say it.

It wasn't that he was interested in her romantically. At least not yet. He hadn't decided how he felt about her in that way.

But she was the easiest person in the house to talk to. She would turn fifteen before he turned seventeen, so they weren't quite two years apart. Lionel was only thirteen and Ryan twelve, so although they were boys, Judd usually chose to talk with Vicki.

But she was gone, at least for a while. He worried about her.

Judd liked having Vicki around because she was a buffer between Lionel and Ryan. They squabbled all the time. Judd told himself he didn't care, but they got on his nerves. He knew they were like brothers and that down deep they liked each other and probably loved each other as brothers in Christ. They just didn't act like it.

Lionel, who had been raised in a Christian home, was a know-it-all who treated Ryan like a dummy. Well, what did Lionel expect from a kid who had hardly been to church? The whole thing made Judd feel old. Here he was, suddenly without parents, and he was worried about people who lived with him and for whom he felt responsible. All this in just a couple of weeks. It was too bizarre.

Vicki feared she had made a mistake as soon as she caught the attention of the driver of an eighteen-wheeler. She had been praying that a family would give her a ride. If not a family, then a couple. If not a couple, then a woman. Vicki hesitated when the truck rumbled onto the shoulder and awaited her approach. She could have easily ignored him, but, after all, she *had* been standing there with her thumb out.

She prayed as she approached the passenger side. At the trailer park she had grown up in, a friend was a truck driver. So she knew how to mount the steps, open the door, and swing herself inside. But with the door open, Vicki froze. This driver was a man, and he already had a passenger—another man. She smelled alcohol and both men held beer cans.

"Well, well, well," the passenger said, "lookie what we got here!"

He was young and blond with close-cropped hair, and he wore a sleeveless tee shirt despite the chilly evening. He offered her his free hand, but she hesitated, one hand on the door handle, the other on the side of the cab. The man smiled and she smelled his breath. "C'mon in, honey. You can sit right here between us."

"Yeah," the driver said. "We'll take a lady like you anywhere you want to go!" He was muscular and sweaty.

"I was, uh, just wondering how far it is to Mount Prospect," Vicki said. There was no way she'd ride with these two.

"You know good and well where it is," the passenger said. "You had your thumb out there, honey. Now, where to?"

"Nowhere," she said and began to step back down.

"No you don't, sweetie," the young man said, and he pushed the door wide open. Vicki hung from the handle and dangled high off the ground. He pulled the door back toward him, and Vicki had to act. The last thing she wanted was to get close enough for him to reach her. She let go and dropped to the ground.

"Thanks anyway," she called out, heading toward the back of the truck as the door shut. But she knew that was not going to satisfy the truckers when the door opened again and the man bounded out, sloshing his beer can as he did.

Vicki slipped in the gravel and tried to run, her heart thundering. She was no match for a man that size. As she desperately prayed she realized how stupid she had been to take off on her own. What had she been thinking?

The man was gaining on her when another truck rolled off the side of the road, the skidding tires kicking up dust. Vicki found herself next to the passenger door of that vehicle as it flew open. Now what?

She was relieved to see this driver was alone and older, probably in his sixties, big, barrel-chested, and with a week's growth of white whiskers. His smile disarmed her.

"You ought to be careful, hitchikin' by yourself these days, little lady," he said.

"Can you help me?" she said.

"What's the trouble?"

She pointed behind her, but when she turned, the young man had turned tail and was climbing back into the other truck. Taking no chances, Vicki leaped aboard the new truck.

"Where you going?" the old trucker said.

"Michigan," she said, noticing a leather cross dangling from the CB radio mounted above the dash.

"I can get you as far as Michigan City, Indiana," he said. "How'll that be?"

"An answer to prayer," she said.

The old man was shifting into one gear after the other every few feet, getting back up to speed as he pulled back onto the road. When he finally had the rig in the right lane and rolling with the heavy traffic, he cocked his head and stared at Vicki.

"Did you say that just to get next to me,

'cause you saw the cross? Or are you really a woman of prayer?"

"I am now," she said.

He chuckled and turned his gaze back at the road. "Aren't we all?" he said. "Call me Deacon."

"Deacon?"

"Yes, ma'am."

"Are you a deacon?"

"Actually no. But once I found the Lord and started telling everybody on the squawk box, they started calling me Deacon. I'm a little zealous I guess you might say."

"Me too."

"You a believer, Miss?"

"Vicki," she said. "With an *I*."

"Well, praise the Lord, Vicki with an *I*. Tell me your story and I'll tell you mine."

Vicki ran down her whole history before Deacon reached the state line. The ride was punctuated by occasional static from the CB radio, words she could just barely make out.

"That you, Deacon?" came one interruption. "This here's the Fat Fox."

"Hey, Fatty, how ya doin', come back."

"Seventy-threes to you, Deke. Still totin' the Lord?"

"That's a big four, Fats. You will be too if you wanna survive the flip side."

"I got the whole sermon the other day,

Deacon," the other man said. "Just saying hey."

"Well, hey back, Fox. Don't be making the Lord wait on you too long now, you hear? I want to be calling you brother next time I see you."

Deacon explained to Vicki that he liked to preach over the citizens' band radio. A lot of drivers were scared and curious since the vanishings. "I take a lot of heat for it from some. They tell me to put a lid on it or save it for Sunday, but it's way too late to be ashamed of God, don't you think?"

Vicki nodded. "Did you not believe before, or did you just not know?"

"I knew. My mother, God rest her soul, told me every day of her life. But I blamed God because she married the wrong man. He treated her wrong. Me too. I hated him till the day he died, and I always thought she deserved better than a man like that. I quit going to church fifty years ago and never went back. She sent me verses and reminders and letters and prayers every month until she died a couple of years ago. I almost got saved at her funeral. I knew what they were saying was the truth, but I figured that if I came to Jesus I would have too much apologizing to do. Three former wives, you know."

Vicki wondered why he thought she'd know.

"Anyway, my last wife became a Christian about six months after she left me. She wanted to come back, make things right, clean me up, get my life straightened out. I didn't want any part of it. She warned me that Jesus would come back and I wouldn't be ready. Boy, was she right! When everybody disappeared, I only needed to know one thing: Was Janice here or gone? As soon as I knew she was gone, leavin' her waitress uniform right where she stood, I knew it was true. I knew what to do, who to pray to, and what to say."

"Me too," Vicki said. "Quit drinking and smoking too."

Deacon tilted his head back and roared with laughter. "You got off the sauce and the cancer sticks when you got saved too, did you?"

"Yes, sir!"

He laughed louder. "Is that a fact?"

"Yes, it is, and I don't think it's funny. Why are you laughing?"

He wiped his eyes and down shifted. "I'm sorry, sweetheart," he said. "You just don't hit me as the hard-livin' type, if you know what I mean."

"You should have seen me three weeks

ago," she said. "I never thought I would look like this, talk like this, or act like this either. Most people called me trailer trash."

"Grew up in a park?"

"Yes, sir. Prospect Gardens."

"I know the place. No garden, is it?"

"Never was. Asphalt and dirt."

"And some indoor/outdoor, right?"

"Sir?"

"That plastic indoor/outdoor carpeting that's supposed to fool people into thinking you've got a yard?"

She laughed. "We sure enough had a slab of that ourselves," she said.

Vicki told him of the trailers that had burned, and of her brother's friend Bub, who had been left behind.

Deacon was quiet for a few miles and appeared thoughtful. "Ever wonder if he doesn't want to be found?" he said finally.

Vicki shrugged. "It doesn't make any difference. It's like God put him in my heart and I have to be sure he knows the truth."

"Not everybody reacts well, you know," Deacon said.

Vicki nodded. "That's OK. I'm just supposed to tell him."

Deacon told her that he wouldn't feel right about leaving her at the Michigan state line, not knowing whether she got a ride to Portage. "I'll sit with you as long as I can at the truck stop there," he said. "I want to make sure you catch a ride with somebody I know and trust."

"Thank you, Deacon," she said.

※

Judd wished Vicki had told him she was going with or without him. He would have at least made her promise to call him once in a while so he'd know she was all right. Now how would he get word to her about school? Loudspeakers began blaring late Friday night, informing residents to tune in certain radio and TV emergency-broadcast stations. "Local schools will reopen a week from tomorrow," came the announcements, "and those stations will carry the details."

"What details?" Ryan said, and he and Lionel joined Judd in front of the TV.

"Listen and find out, stupid," Lionel said.

"I just figured you'd know, genius," Ryan said.

"Knock it off, you two," Judd said. "I want to hear this."

"We already know what they're going to say," Lionel said. "We know when, we know where, and we know what. School. Yuck."

"You both go to Lincoln, right?" Judd said. Lionel nodded.

"Me too," Ryan said. "But we're not in the same classes."

"At least I have *something* to be thankful for," Lionel said.

Judd shushed them as the list of schools came up. As the names of junior highs scrolled past, Judd read, "Formerly Lincoln Junior High, now Global Community Middle School."

Lionel seemed to flinch. "Why would they do that?" he said. "Change a perfectly good name. I liked going to a school named after a great president."

The phone rang.

"I'll get it," Ryan said. Judd let him as he watched the high school listings. But the station did better than just list the openings. The news of Prospect High was accompanied by film footage of the changing of the sign out front.

"It's for you," Ryan said from the kitchen phone. "Judd!"

Judd heard him but didn't respond. He stood, staring at the screen. A cherry picker and crane on the back of a truck hoisted a workman to the Prospect High sign. As Ryan nagged him from the kitchen, Judd saw the man on TV trade one sheet of plastic for another that slid in front of the lights on the sign.

Prospect High was no longer. His school would now be known as Nicolae Carpathia High. The sports mascot would also be changed. The teams formerly known as the Knights would now be the Doves.

"C'mon, Judd!" Ryan whined. "It's Bruce for you."

TWO

The Announcement

"You been watching the news?" Bruce asked.

"Yes," Judd said, "unfortunately."

"You understand what's going on?"

"What's to understand? School starts a week from tomorrow at Nicolae Carpathia High."

Bruce laughed. "Well, it may come to that, but I meant—"

"What do you mean it *may* come to that? I was serious." Judd told him of the school announcements.

"It doesn't surprise me about their changing Lincoln to Global Community," Bruce said. "That's going to happen everywhere with the new emphasis on a one-world government. They'll want to remove nationalism and make everything planet oriented. But to already start naming things after the UN secretary-general? Wow."

"I thought you were calling to make sure I knew school was back on," Judd said.

"No, you caught that before I did. I just finished a meeting with the adult core group I told you about—the Tribulation Force."

"Yeah, the pilot and his daughter?"

"And the magazine writer. Anyway, they had not heard the big international news today, and I wanted to make sure you heard it. I have to prepare my Sunday sermon tomorrow morning, but I wondered if you four would want to come to my office early so we could talk about it."

"Three of us can. What's the news?"

"Carpathia is making himself unavailable for several days while he and his top people work on what he calls 'an understanding' between the global community and Israel, and a special arrangement between the UN and the United States."

"What does that mean?"

"That's what I'd like to talk to the Junior Trib Force about tomorrow. Sorry, the Kids Trib Force."

"How about we just call it the Young Trib Force?" Judd said.

"Sure," Bruce said. "Now, who can't make it?"

When Judd told Bruce where Vicki was, Judd was met with a long silence. "Judd," the pastor said finally, "this is not going to work."

Judd felt his neck flush. "What's not going to work?"

"You being in charge of these kids. If you can't control—"

"Controlling them is not my job!" Judd blurted. "I'm just giving them a place to stay. I'm not their parent. I can't tell them what to do."

"Judd, listen to me. I feel responsible for you guys too, because I know you and know where you are. You'd never get away with living alone at your ages if we weren't in the middle of a crisis. If the police weren't so busy, they'd never stand for this. I ought to call them and have them watch for Vicki, and if they don't have the manpower, I should be out looking for her myself. Where is she headed?"

"I'm not sure," Judd said, "but you're not responsible for us. We don't answer to you, and we don't have to do what you say. What are you going to do? Tell on us? Get us in trouble? What kind of a friend is that?"

Judd couldn't believe he was talking that way to a man he admired and respected as much as he did Bruce Barnes. Bruce had led all four of the kids to Christ and treated them with respect. But Judd didn't like to be lectured or told what to do. Now he sensed he had hurt Bruce, who was silent again.

"I'd like to think I'm your pastor," Bruce said at last. Judd felt guilty when he heard the emotion in Bruce's voice. He had broken the man's heart, and he knew he should apologize. Judd didn't have much experience with that, but he knew he would have to get around to it sometime soon. "Will you at least come early tomorrow morning so I can tell you what I think about what's going on?"

"Of course," Judd said, trying to sound encouraging and apologetic. "How early?"

"Like I said, I've got sermon preparation, so if you could come as early as eight, I'd appreciate it."

"We'll be there," Judd said. "All of us who are here anyway."

"You don't mind telling the younger ones what to do?"

Judd knew he had been caught in his own weak logic.

Deacon looked at his watch. Vicki was aware that they had been getting puzzled stares from other truckers as they ate at the counter in the truck stop. Deacon insisted on paying, though she told him she had borrowed plenty of money from Judd.

"Don't be saying that too loud either," he said. "You don't want anybody knowing you're carrying a lot of cash."

"Hey, Deacon," a man said on his way out. "Keep preachin', bro."

"Will do, Claud. Hey, you're not runnin' to Michigan tonight, are you?"

"Nope, sorry. What's up?"

"Looking for a ride for a friend. Can't let her ride with just anybody."

"But you'd trust her with me?" Claud said, smiling at Vicki. "I'm flattered. If you want to see Pennsylvania tomorrow, you can ride with me, little lady. Otherwise, I can't help ya."

"Thanks anyway," Vicki said.

Deacon checked the time again. "I've got to get going soon," he said, "but tell me something. Did you say your boyfriend had wheels?"

She nodded. "He's not my boyfriend."

"But he took you and the other two in, so he's a good friend?"

"You could say that."

"I need you to do me a favor, Vicki. Would you?"

"Depends."

"I want you to call your friend and have him come get you. Now don't shake your head. Hear me out. I don't think it's an accident you wound up riding in my truck tonight. I think God put us together to protect you."

"Believe me, I can take care of myself."

"Little lady, I can't even take care of *my*self

in this new day, and I'm a big, old, ugly man. Who knows what kind of trouble you could get yourself into out there? Now I have to go, but I'm not leaving until I know you've got a ride home."

"But I have to get to—"

"Let me finish. I promise I'll check with some people I know, people in law enforcement who can track this guy down for you, make sure he's all right."

"But I need to talk to him face-to-face. He treats me like a little girl and wouldn't listen to me on the phone. If I was right there, he couldn't just blow me off."

"Well, then one of these days, when I know far enough in advance that I'm going to Michigan from the west, I'll let you know and you can go with me."

Vicki sat back and stared at Deacon. "You'd do that for me?"

He nodded. "What's a brother for?"

Judd was relieved to hear from Vicki, so much so that he didn't even mind the trip in the middle of the night to get her. He was not happy, however, to discover that she had given their phone number to Deacon. He seemed like a harmless and wonderful old guy, but who knew who was for real these days?

Judd was stony on the way home. Vicki badgered him to find out what was wrong.

"Bruce says this isn't working," he said, "and when you pull a stunt like this, I wonder if he might be right."

Vicki shook her head as if she was frustrated and angry. "So kick me out of the house," she said. "We don't answer to Bruce. At least I don't. And I don't answer to you either. I mean, I'm grateful for all you've done, but you're not my mom or dad."

"You didn't obey *them* either," Judd said, and he knew he had gone too far this time. "Well," he added, trying to make it better, "you told me that yourself."

THREE

Meeting with Bruce

VICKI could hardly believe herself. How could she be talking like that to the one person who had made her life bearable? She believed she had made Judd say something crueler than he had intended. The worst of it was that he was right. She was starting to talk to Judd and about Bruce the same way she had talked to and about her parents. Yet now she missed them with an ache so deep she knew it would not be soothed until she saw them with Jesus.

She wanted to apologize, but the words would not come. Bruce had taught the kids about having to deal with their old selves, their sin natures. Now she was discovering what he meant. Vicki had endured Lionel's and Ryan's bickering, passing that off as childishness and blaming it on their ages. But she and Judd should have known better. How could they let their old natures take over after all God, and Bruce, had done for them?

What had the encounter with Deacon been all about if not God showing her that he would protect her even when she did something stupid? Vicki had felt free and powerful when she started out, walking from the house out of the neighborhood and onto the main roads leading to the expressway. But then fear and foreboding had overtaken her, and she felt tense every second. Only when she finally saw Judd and was safely in his car and on the way back to the house did she realize how afraid she had been. Why couldn't she say that? Pride? Resentment at having been scolded, in essence, by both Judd and Bruce?

She opened her mouth to say something, anything, but Judd beat her to it.

"I'm sorry, Vicki," he said. "I shouldn't have said that. I don't know why I do that. I care about you, that's all. I really thought it was a bad idea for you to go to Michigan at all, but if I had known you were going to do it anyway, I'd have taken you."

"You would've?"

"Of course! I haven't been able to sleep or do anything, wondering about you, worrying about you."

She put a hand on his arm. "You're sounding more and more like a parent all the time."

"I know," he said, smiling. "And I can't believe it."

Vicki felt Judd tense under her touch and quickly pulled her hand away. She didn't want to give him the wrong idea. She appreciated him. She liked him. But getting really interested in him, interested that way, would be a mistake.

"I'm sorry too, Judd," she said. "I feel rotten when I act so selfish. I think I had the right idea, wanting to find Bub. God really did put that in my heart. But going myself was just trying to show you I was independent or something—I don't know. It's just that I feel this desperation to tell everybody about God. There's been enough death. Nobody should still wonder what the disappearances were all about."

"I know," Judd said. "Maybe this Deacon guy can get you in touch with Bub somehow. You'll get your chance."

"I hope so."

Judd told her about the school announcements.

"Oh, brother," she said. "That sure seems like a waste of time. Aren't you going to feel squirrelly, sitting in school while the rest of the world is dying?"

He nodded but didn't say anything.

"What?" she said. "You don't agree? I mean, what will we be studying and why? I was never that good a student, but I knew I needed that diploma to get any kind of job. School was all about the future. Well, now there is no future like that, so what's the point?"

Judd was still quiet, and Vicki was intrigued. Usually she could tell when he agreed with her, and now he didn't seem to. "You going?" she said. "Back to school, I mean?"

He nodded.

"You're going to be a Carpathia Dove?"

"That I'll never be," he said, "but, yeah, I'm going to go."

"You mind saying why?"

"For the same reasons you're talking about."

"The future?"

He nodded.

"But don't you agree you'll be studying subjects you'll never use? Whatever kind of job you'll have will have nothing to do with what you learn in high school now."

He nodded again. Vicki sensed herself getting mad again. "So, why waste your time?" she said.

"I told you," he said. "The future. Everybody at that high school needs to know what we know. You'd rather be out telling everybody about Jesus, but what about all those kids we'll see every day? They were left behind just like we were. We'll probably meet some believers, but I'll bet not many."

He had a point. "But will we be allowed to tell them about God?" she said. "Especially if Carpathia *is* the Antichrist? I can't imagine anyone letting us do that in a building named after the guy himself. And what kind of sense does it make that we go to a school with that name?"

Judd pulled into the driveway. "It's going to seem weird," he said. "I don't guess I'll be buying a varsity jacket."

He told Vicki about the morning meeting with Bruce, then let her out of the car before pulling into the garage. "Thanks for coming to get me, Judd. I didn't deserve it."

"Yeah," he said. "Well, you're grounded."

She was too tired to smile.

Judd, on the other hand, was unable to sleep. He wandered into his father's den, where the latest monster computer sat. Judd and Marc and Marcie used to play games on it and surf the Net. Judd had enjoyed all the chat rooms, though his parents warned him about the worst ones. Those didn't even tempt him now.

He pulled the dustcover off and fired up the machine. He was stunned to see how many advertisements he found for people with schemes on how to get rich in light of the global mess. One ghastly Web site promised a listing of everybody who had died or disappeared. Judd spent an hour there, pulling up names of his own family and other acquaintances to see how accurate the thing was.

His parents were listed as having disappeared. Ryan's parents were listed as known dead. Vicki's parents were listed as killed in a trailer fire, which he knew was not true but would also be impossible to prove. Judd wanted to look up Bub for Vicki, but that wasn't enough to go on. Bub couldn't be his real first name, and even if it was, Judd had never heard a last name. Vicki had to know it, though, because she gave Deacon enough info that he was sure he could track down Eddie Byrne's friend.

Judd was amazed to see how late it was. He had promised Bruce he would bring at least Lionel and Ryan to the church in the morning. Vicki would be a pleasant surprise for Bruce.

The phone awakened Judd, and he was star-
tled to notice that it was already ten minutes
after eight. "Oh, no," he groaned, knowing
the caller would be Bruce. He was right, and
he quickly apologized, promising to get
everybody rounded up and over there as fast
as he could. Judd explained he had been up
late, going to get Vicki.

"At least that's good news," Bruce said.
"Now please respect my schedule so I can get
to my sermon preparation when I need to."

Judd scolded Lionel and Ryan for not getting him up, but they, of course, blamed
each other. "You never told me when the
meeting was," Vicki said, sitting at the table
in the kitchen. "I'm ready when you are."

Twenty minutes later, after Judd's shower,
they all piled into the car. No surprise to Judd,
Bruce seemed perturbed when they arrived.
He didn't lecture them, but he did say he was
willing to have a regular meeting time every
other day and that they would be expected to
be there on time and ready to study. "There's
so much for you to learn, and if you're going
to back to school, you're going to be in the
minority there. It won't be easy."

He prayed and then opened his Bible, but
before saying anything, he took a deep

breath and seemed on the verge of tears. "I feel a tremendous responsibility for you all," he said. "I know you don't want me to. You want to be independent and not answer to anyone. We're all that way. But it's nothing but pride and selfishness. The Bible says that as your pastor, I am also your shepherd. That doesn't make me your parent, but if you want to be in the church and in this little group, your responsibility is to respect my authority over you.

"That's not easy for me either. I'm not used to it yet myself. I'm trying to run this church, but I'm also spending most of my days and evenings studying the Bible and commentaries so I can try to explain to you and everyone else what is going on."

"And what's to come," Judd offered.

"Exactly. I feel the press of God on me. It's hard. And I know I'm not the only one who feels it. We're all hurting, we've all lost people, we all missed the truth. I don't want to lay this all on you, but my house is so big and so cold and so lonely without my family that sometimes I don't even go home at night. I study here until I fall asleep, and I go home in the morning only to clean up and change and get back here."

Judd didn't know what to say. He hadn't seen Bruce like this. One thing was for sure:

Judd wouldn't let anybody be late to these meetings again.

"One of the things I had never been good at was reading the Bible every day," Bruce continued. "I pretended to be a believer, a so-called full-time Christian worker, but I didn't care about the Bible. Now I can't get enough of it. I know what people meant when they used to say they feasted on the Word. Sometimes I sit drinking it in for hours, losing track of time, weeping and praying, forgetting to eat. Sometimes I just slip from my chair and fall to my knees, calling out to God to make it clear to me. Most frightening—and thrilling—of all, he's doing just that."

Vicki was riveted, and she could tell even the younger boys were too. They hadn't seen Bruce like this. Something was weighing on him, and it had nothing to do with the fact that the Young Trib Force had been late that Saturday morning.

"I need your prayers," Bruce continued. "God is showing me things, impressing truth on me that I can barely keep quiet about. Yet if I say these things publicly, I will be ridiculed and might even be in danger."

"Like what?" Vicki said.

Bruce stepped to the corner of his desk and sat on it, towering over the kids. "We know

Nicolae Carpathia is the Antichrist. Even if the story Mr. Williams told you about Carpathia's supernatural hypnotic power and his murder of those two men was not true—and of course I believe it is—there's still plenty of evidence against him. He fits the prophecies. He's deceptive. He's charming. People are drawn to him, flocking to support him. He has been thrust into power, seemingly against his own wishes. He's pushing a one-world government, a one-world money system, a treaty with Israel, moving the UN to Babylon. That alone proves it."

Vicki's ears perked up at the mention of the treaty with Israel. "He's said that?" she said. "On the news, I mean? Isn't that the start of the seven-year tribulation?"

Bruce nodded. "Yesterday," he said. "His spokesman said Carpathia would be unavailable for several days while he conducted strategic high-level meetings."

"But did he say what they would be about?"

"He said Carpathia felt obligated to move quickly to unite the world in a move toward peace. He's having nations destroy 90 percent of their weaponry and donate the remaining 10 percent to the UN in Babylon, which he has renamed New Babylon. He's also pushing the international money people to settle on one form of currency for the whole world. And he wants all the religions of the world to unite as one big group that tolerates everybody's beliefs. I'm guessing we'll see a one-world religion."

Vicki's mind was reeling, as it had been since the day of the disappearances. At times she still wondered if this was some crazy nightmare. In an instant she had gone from a rebellious teenager to a fanatical believer in Christ. She wanted to press Bruce, to ask him about this treaty. That would be proof, if nothing else was, but how did he know? She didn't want to interrupt him.

"All I know," he was saying, "is that the closer I get to God, the deeper I get into the Bible, the heavier the burden seems on my shoulders. The world needs to know it is being deceived. I feel an urgency to preach Christ everywhere, not just here. This church is full of frightened people, and they're hungry for God. We're trying to meet that need, but more trouble is coming."

When he paused, Vicki jumped in. "But the treaty. Has he really announced a treaty?"

Bruce looked at her and nodded. "The news that really got to me yesterday was the announcement that the next major order of business for Carpathia is what he calls 'an understanding' between the global community and Israel. I don't know what form it will take or what the benefit will be to the Holy Land, but clearly this is the seven-year treaty. If that announcement says anything about a promise from Carpathia that Israel will be protected over the next seven years, it officially ushers in the Tribulation."

FOUR

Back Home

"CAN we go soon?" Ryan asked. "I have no idea what you guys are talking about."

"Figure it out, short stuff," Lionel said. "It's only the end of the world."

Bruce leaned forward. "I understand you two haven't been getting along," he said. "Lionel, you know this stuff, don't you? Better than Ryan, I mean?"

"'Course," Lionel said. "Doesn't everybody?"

"And is that his fault?"

"No. I was raised in church. He wasn't."

"So he's not stupid or a dummy?"

"Unless he doesn't want to learn."

"And I think he does, especially if he understands what we're talking about. You should teach him."

"Why me?"

"You're closest to his age," Bruce said. "He listens to you whether you think so or not. It's important that you're positive. He acts like he's mad at you, and sometimes maybe he doesn't like you because you keep putting him down. But he needs you, and he would look up to you if you treated him better."

Lionel looked down, and Judd hoped Bruce was getting through to him. It was a good idea—Lionel's being Ryan's teacher. The question was whether either of them would tolerate it.

"You two work it out," Bruce said.

Lionel rolled his head to gaze at Ryan, who looked back with brows raised. Judd took that to mean that both were willing to give it a try. Now that could be interesting.

Judd missed his parents and his little brother and sister, and he knew the others missed their families too. But he was excited about doing something positive, not sitting around feeling sorry for himself. They had only a few years left, and he wanted to see their group be just as eager to stand and fight as the adult Tribulation Force.

"Bruce," he said, raising his hand. "Do you have time for us, with all the other stuff you're doing, I mean?"

"I'll make the time if you'll all get serious about it. The adult Force meets here every night for two hours. I can meet with you guys after school whenever possible. I'll outline what God has revealed in the Bible. If

I'm right and if the treaty with Israel comes within the next few days, we have no time to waste. I want this church to start new churches, new groups of believers. I want to go to Israel and hear the two witnesses preach at the Wailing Wall. Imagine the stories I'll come back with. By the way, you know there's a place on the Internet where you can watch what's happening at the Wall twenty-four hours a day."

"Yippee," Lionel said, and Bruce looked hard at him.

"Just kiddin'," Lionel said, "but isn't most of that in Jewish?"

Bruce smiled. "Their language is Hebrew, but often there are subtitles or even interpreters. You might find it interesting, especially when the witnesses are preaching. The Bible foretells of 144,000 Jews springing up and traveling throughout the world to preach the gospel. There will be a great soul harvest, maybe a billion or more people, coming to Christ."

"Wow!" Judd said. "Does it say there'll be that many?"

"Well, this is a good study for you. Lionel, grab that King James Bible over there. Thanks. Usually we use the New King James, or the New International, or the New Living Translation, so we can understand it better.

But let's look at this in an older version and see if we can figure it out. Ryan, find Revelation 9:16, and read it to us."

Ryan took the Bible from Lionel, and Judd was pleased to hear Lionel whisper, "Last book in the whole Bible."

Ryan found the verse and read, "'And the number of the army of the horsemen were two hundred thousand thousand: and I heard the number of them.'"

"Stop there," Bruce said. "What was the number he heard?"

"Me?" Ryan said.

"If you know."

"Anybody knows that," he said. "A thousand thousand is a million, so the number he heard was two hundred million."

"Good," Bruce said. "Now, at the risk of being too simple, would you say that army of horsemen, even though it was two hundred million, could be counted?"

"Of course," Ryan said. "The number's right here."

"Right. It's obvious. So, Judd, read Revelation 7:9."

Judd took the Bible from Ryan and read, "'After this I beheld, and, lo, a great multitude, which no man could number, of all nations, and kindreds, and people, and tongues, stood before the throne, and before the Lamb, clothed with white robes, and palms in their hands.'"

"That's enough," Bruce said. "Anybody catch it?"

Vicki said, "I don't know who they're talking about, but it's a crowd so big nobody can number it."

"Exactly. That's how we know there will be a huge soul harvest. This is talking about people who come to Christ during the Tribulation. If an army of two hundred million can be counted, how many must there be in a crowd no man can number?"

Judd stole a glance at Ryan, who looked excited. "Is all this stuff this interesting?" Ryan said.

"That's nothing," Bruce said. "You'll be as amazed as I have been with what's in here."

"All those people becoming believers," Vicki said. "We should be thrilled."

"I *am*," Bruce said. "But we're not going to have much time to celebrate and certainly no time to rest. Remember the seven Seal Judgments Revelation talks about?"

"You said something about them, yes."

"Those will begin with the signing of the treaty. There will be eighteen months of peace, but in the three months after that—twenty-one months into the eighty-four-month Tribulation—the rest of the Seal

Judgments will fall on the earth. One-fourth of the world's population will be wiped out. Do you understand what that means?"

"One-fourth of the people who have been left behind?" Lionel said.

Bruce nodded.

"I don't like the odds," Judd said. "There are four of us kids."

"One of us is going to die before even two years are up?"

Bruce didn't say anything. Judd saw him just looking at them, one by one.

"Whew!" Ryan said. "Maybe some of this isn't that interesting after all. I mean, it's interesting, but it's like stuff you don't really want to know."

"I want to know about it," Vicki said, speaking louder and more quickly than Judd had heard her before. "I want to know everything, every detail. There's no guarantee I won't be the one who's killed by the twenty-first month. I want to make sure I'm doing everything I'm supposed to be doing in the meantime."

"To earn your way to heaven," Bruce said. "Right?"

"Right! I mean, no! I know better, Bruce. I know I can't earn my way. I just want to do the right thing because it's the right thing. Millions of people are going to die in the first quarter of the Tribulation, so we have to tell them the truth as fast as we can."

"That's what I like to hear. One of the adults last night said the same thing. He said, 'We don't want to just survive; we want to take action.'"

Now they were talking Judd's language, and he was thrilled that they all seemed excited about it. There was a reason God had put them together, and they were going to do important things for him.

Vicki raised her hand. "How many people will be left at the end?"

"When Jesus returns again," Bruce said, "at the Glorious Appearing?" She nodded. "With all the judgments—fourteen more following the seven Seal Judgments—there will be war and famine and pestilence and plagues. My study tells me that several of the judgments wipe out another third of the population. That's a third of the three-fourths who are left, then a third of the two-thirds left after that, and so on. It's confusing, but if you put a calculator to it, it looks like only one of every four people who were left at the Rapture will be left standing at the Glorious Appearing."

"The rest will be in heaven or hell?" Ryan said.

"Right. And the ones in heaven will return

with Christ to set up his earthly kingdom, his thousand-year reign."

Ryan looked at the others. "I'd like to be the one left standing, but if I'm not, I get to go to heaven *and* come back? That would be cool too."

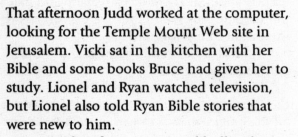

That afternoon Judd worked at the computer, looking for the Temple Mount Web site in Jerusalem. Vicki sat in the kitchen with her Bible and some books Bruce had given her to study. Lionel and Ryan watched television, but Lionel also told Ryan Bible stories that were new to him.

Late in the afternoon, Lionel hollered up the stairs. "Hey, Judd, some guy on TV is talking about announcements from the UN and all that. You want to hear it?"

"I do!" Vicki said, emerging from the kitchen.

Judd joined the others in front of the TV, where a commentator said: "Moving the UN out of New York and into the ruins of Babylon, south of Baghdad, is a good thing. If Carpathia is sincere about disarming the world and stockpiling the remaining 10 percent of the weapons, I'd rather he store them in the Middle East than on an island off New York City.

"But the world will never settle on a single religion, and as streamlined as it may be, there will never be fewer than three currencies either."

"What are currencies?" Ryan asked.

"Types of money," Judd said. "Like now we have American dollars, European marks, and Asian yen. Carpathia wants to go to just dollars. Bruce thinks eventually Carpathia wants to go to no cash."

"How would they do that?"

"Everybody would have an account and a credit card. Anything you want, you just put on that card. No cash."

"Cool!"

"Yeah," Vicki said, "but what happens when they do away with the card and put a chip or a mark on you to be scanned?"

"Even better," Ryan said. "Nothing to carry."

"But these books Bruce lent me say it will be the mark of the beast, the Antichrist, and then he'll own you. It's right in the Bible."

"Not me," Ryan said. "They'd have to kill me first, so then I'd be in heaven."

As Vicki headed back to the kitchen and Judd toward the stairs, she told him, "Bruce says the only woman in the adult Tribulation Force is the daughter of the pilot."

"I know."

"And she's memorizing three books of the Bible."

"I didn't know *that*."

"She's going to be Bruce's research assistant and help him teach. Maybe she'll teach us when he's out of town."

"That'd be neat. What's she memorizing?"

"The three books with the most end-times prophecies: Ezekiel, Daniel, and Revelation."

"Those are not short books."

"No kidding. But what a goal. Maybe I'll try that. It would be more important than school. But you're right. If I want to tell people, there are going to be a lot of people to tell at Prospect, I mean Nicolae High."

"Nine more days and we're back to class," Judd said.

"I'm looking forward to tomorrow morning. Bruce says he's got a message that excites him. This is so weird. He told me that this woman, Chloe Steele is her name, said she never thought the Bible would interest her, and now she's reading it like there's no tomorrow. Get it?"

"Huh?"

"Like there's no tomorrow. There aren't many, are there?"

Back in his dad's den, Judd sat thinking. Bruce had told Vicki about Chloe Steele, and he had told Judd about Buck Williams, the magazine writer. On the way out of church, Bruce had told Judd the latest thing Buck had told him. "He said he found himself turning to the Gospels rather than the Old Testament or the Revelation prophecies. He was surprised to see what a revolutionary Jesus turned out to be."

"A revolutionary?" Judd had asked.

"You know this stuff as well as I do," Bruce had said. "You grew up with it. Buck is just learning the character, the personality, the mission of Jesus, and it fascinates him. He told me that the Jesus he had always imagined or thought he knew was an impostor. The Jesus of the Bible turns out to be a radical, a man of paradoxes. Jesus said if you want to be rich, give your money away. If you want to be exalted, humble yourself. Revenge sounds logical, but it's wrong. Love your enemies, pray for those who put you down. That kind of thing."

Judd couldn't argue with that. He only wished he'd become a radical Christian long before.

FIVE

The Message

JUDD insisted that everyone in the house be up early and ready to go long before church Sunday morning. No one grumbled. They had somehow turned a corner and were now excited and bold about the task before them. Even Ryan and Lionel seemed to be getting along.

Judd asked that they find good seats in the sanctuary, which was already filling, and he hurried down to the office to see Bruce. Loretta, Bruce's kindly old secretary, was just arriving. She told Judd he could knock on Bruce's door.

"If it can wait, I'd appreciate it," Bruce called out.

"OK," Judd said. "Sorry." But as he walked away, Bruce came to the door. He looked disheveled, unshaven, as if he had stayed up all night.

"I didn't know it was you, Judd. What's up?"

"Nothin'," Judd said. "Just wanted to say hi."

"Glad you did. Pray for me."

"OK, but why?"

"Just feeling the responsibility of this church. Big crowd already?"

Judd nodded. "Jammed. Cars lined up around the block. People mostly look scared or sad."

"They're terrified," Bruce said. "They come here looking for hope, for answers, for God. Some are finding him, and the word is spreading. I've been studying all night. I've got to shave and get going here. You study those verses I suggested?"

"Yeah. I found the one about the quarter of the population."

"Memorize it?"

"Yup."

"Let me hear it."

"You have time?" Judd said.

"Did you really memorize it?"

Judd had to prove it. "Revelation 6:8," he began, "'So I looked, and behold, a pale horse. And the name of him who sat on it was Death, and Hades followed with him. And power was given to them over a fourth of the earth, to kill with sword, with hunger, with death, and by the beasts of the earth.'"

"Excellent, Judd. You're a good student.

Unfortunately, you're going to learn that what comes after the pale horse is worse and keeps getting worse until the end."

***

Vicki waited with Ryan and Lionel in the third pew from the front, in the center row. She saved a seat for Judd. When she saw him coming, she also recognized Buck Williams across the way. He had slid in behind a tall, dark man and a pretty young woman, and they were greeting each other.

"Ryan," she whispered, "don't make a big scene, but is that Captain Steele and his daughter over there in front of Mr. Williams?"

Ryan stood to look, and Vicki cringed. "Yep," he said. "That's them. Mr. S. and Chloe."

Judd joined the kids as the music began.

He noticed that many people didn't know the songs. The words were projected on the wall, and the choruses were simple and catchy, but they were new to some people. As for those, like himself, who knew the words, he wondered how he and they had all missed the truth while singing songs like those.

Finally Bruce hurried to the pulpit—not the large one on the platform, but a small lectern at floor level. He carried his Bible, two large books, and a sheaf of papers he had trouble controlling. He smiled sheepishly.

"Good morning," he began. "I realize a word of explanation is in order. Usually we sing more, but we don't have time for that today. Usually my tie is straighter, my shirt fully tucked in, my suit coat buttoned. That all seems a little less critical this morning. Usually we take up an offering. Be assured we still need it, but please find the baskets on your way out at noon, if I indeed let you out that early.

"I want to take the extra time this morning because I feel an urgency greater even than the last few weeks. I don't want you to worry about me. I haven't become a wild-eyed madman, a cultist, or anything other than what I have been since I realized I had missed the Rapture. I have read more, prayed more, and studied more this week than ever, and I am eager to tell you what God has told me."

Bruce told his own story yet again, how he had lived a phony life for years, even as a member of the pastoral staff. When Jesus came back, Bruce had been left behind, without his wife and precious children. Judd had heard the story, but it still made him want to cry. People all over the church sobbed.

"I never want to stop telling what Christ has done for me," Bruce said. "I will never

again be ashamed of the gospel of Christ.
The Bible says that the Cross offends. If you
are offended, I am doing my job. If you are
attracted to Christ, the Holy Spirit is working.

"We've already missed the Rapture, and
now we live in what will soon become the
most perilous period of history. Evangelists
used to warn people that they could be
struck by a car or die in a fire, and thus they
should not put off coming to Christ. I'm telling you that should a car strike you or a fire
consume you, it may be the most merciful
way you can die. Be ready this time. Be ready.
I will tell you how to get ready."

Bruce announced that his sermon title was
"The Four Horsemen of the Apocalypse" and
that he wanted to concentrate on the rider of
the first horse—the white one.

Judd had never seen him so earnest, so
inspired. As Bruce spoke he referred to his
notes, to the books he'd brought, and to the
Bible. He often wiped sweat from his brow.
Judd noticed that most people were taking
notes and that everyone was following along
in the Bible.

Bruce explained that the book of Revelation spoke of what was to come after Christ
had raptured his church. "Does anyone
doubt we're in the last days?" he thundered.
"Millions disappear, and then what? Some

believe the tribulation period has already begun and that it began with the Rapture. We feel the trials and tribulations from the disappearances of our loved ones, don't we? But that is nothing compared to what is to come.

"During these seven years, God will pour out three consecutive sets of judgments—seven seals in a scroll, seven trumpets, and seven bowls. If the Rapture didn't get your attention, the judgments will. And if the judgments don't, you're going to die apart from God. Horrible as these judgments are, I urge you to see them as final warnings from a loving God who is not willing that any should perish."

Judd was struck to remember that he had heard old Pastor Billings preach on these same subjects. Judd had scoffed and quit listening. It all sounded too weird, too far-fetched, too unbelievable.

"I warn you," Bruce rumbled on several minutes later, "this is not for the faint of heart. Revelation 6:1-2 says, 'Now I saw when the Lamb opened one of the seals; and I heard one of the four living creatures saying with a voice like thunder, "Come and see." And I looked, and behold, a white horse. He who sat on it had a bow; and a crown was given to him, and he went out conquering and to conquer.'"

Bruce stepped back and began clearing off the lectern. "Don't worry," he said, "I'm not finished." People applauded. Bruce said, "Are you clapping because you want me to finish, or because you want me to go on all afternoon?"

The people clapped all the more, including the Young Tribulation Force. If the others were like Judd, they were drinking this in, and they wanted more and more. Clearly Bruce had been in tune with what God was showing him. He said over and over that this was not new truth, that the commentaries he cited were decades old, and that the doctrine of the end times was much, much older than that. But those who had said such teaching was not to be taken literally, well, they had been left behind. All of a sudden it was all right to take Scripture at its word! If nothing else convinced people, losing so many to the Rapture had finally reached them.

Bruce stood before the bare lectern now with only his Bible in his hand. "I want to tell you now what I believe the Bible is saying about the rider of the white horse, the first horseman of the Apocalypse. I will not give my opinion. I will not draw any conclusions. I will simply leave it to God to help you draw any parallels that need to be drawn. I *will* tell you this in advance: This millenniums-old account reads as fresh to me as tomorrow's newspaper."

Vicki couldn't believe an hour had flown by since she'd last checked her watch. She was hungry, but she could sit there all day listening to Bruce. She knew where he was going with this imagery, but more amazing, she knew someone in the sanctuary right then who knew the rider of the white horse personally. Buck Williams had experienced the power of the Antichrist. Buck had convinced her that Nicolae Carpathia was the man, the enemy of God.

"Notice," Bruce continued, "that it is the Lamb who opens the first seal and reveals that horseman. The Lamb is Jesus Christ, the Son of God, who died for our sins, was resurrected, and recently raptured his church.

"Who is this first horseman? Clearly he represents the Antichrist and his kingdom. His purpose is 'conquering and to conquer.' He has a bow in his hand, a symbol of warfare, and yet there is no mention of an arrow. How will he conquer? Other passages say he is a 'willful king' and that he will win through smooth talking. He will usher in a false peace, promising world unity. Will he be victorious? Yes! He has a crown.

"The rider of the white horse is the Antichrist, who comes as a deceiver promising peace and uniting the world. The Old Testament says he will sign a treaty with Israel. He will appear to be their friend and protector, but in the end he will be their conqueror and destroyer."

Bruce said he could prove that he himself was not the Antichrist—not that anyone suspected him—because he would never promise peace. "The Bible is clear that we will have a year and a half of peace following the pact with Israel. But in the long run, I predict the opposite of peace. The other three horsemen are coming, and they bring war, famine, plagues, and death. That is not a popular message, not a warm fuzzy you can cling to this week. Our only hope is in Christ, and even in him we will likely suffer."

Bruce closed in prayer, and Vicki assumed everyone else felt as she did, that she could have stayed all day. She tried to get to Bruce, but he had already been intercepted in the aisle, near the Steeles. Vicki was behind him as people quizzed him.

"Are you saying Nicolae Carpathia is the Antichrist?" one said.

"Did you hear me say that?" Bruce said.

"No, but it was pretty clear. They're already talking on the news about his plans and some sort of a deal with Israel."

"Keep reading and studying," Bruce said.

"But it can't be Carpathia, can it? Does he strike you as a liar?"

"How does he strike you?" Bruce said.

"As a savior."

"Almost like a messiah?" Bruce pressed.

"Yeah!"

"There is only one Savior, one Messiah."

"I know, spiritually, but politically I mean. Don't tell me Carpathia's not what he seems to be."

"I'll tell you only what Scripture says," Bruce said, "and I urge you to listen carefully to the news. We must be wise as serpents and gentle as doves."

"That's how I would have described Carpathia," a woman said.

"Be careful," Bruce said, "about giving Christlike characteristics to anyone who doesn't align himself with Christ."

Vicki had been stopped by Bruce's comment about being wise and gentle. She couldn't wait to tell the rest of the Young Trib Force about that. Wise and gentle was what they had to be when they went back to school. So many people needed what the

Young Trib Force had to offer, and yet so much danger awaited them too.

The four were strangely silent on the way home, and Vicki assumed that was because they had all been so moved by Bruce and his sermon. They ate as if they hadn't eaten for hours—which was true. Just before Vicki finished, the phone rang. Ryan, who loved to answer it, announced it was for her.

"Guy named Deacon," Ryan whispered. "Sounds old."

SIX

Deacon and Bub

"THIS Bub guy," Deacon said, "you know him well?"

"Never met him," Vicki said. "I told you. He was a friend of my brother's."

"You sure you got his name right? Beryl Gaylor, right?"

"Right. Why?"

"Are you sitting down?"

"Just tell me."

"He's dead, Vicki. When did you say you talked to him last?"

Vicki could hardly speak. "The day of the Rapture," she managed. "He was fine. What happened?"

"Here's what I heard from my friend in the police department," Deacon said. "Gaylor was missing for a few days, so they searched his and your brother's apartment. They already knew Edward—that's your brother's name, right?"

"Right."

"Had disappeared out of his car. There was no evidence Bub had disappeared, no pile of clothes, that kind of a thing. His answering machine had a message from a friend, asking him to come over and check the friend's basement with him. This guy reported a gas leak the night before. The gas company repairman came out to check the lines in the basement, and then told Bub's friend to find another place to stay for the night while he worked on it. When the guy called the gas company in the morning to see if he could move back in, he couldn't get through—you know, with the vanishings and everything.

"So he was asking Gaylor to go with him to see if his house was OK. The police went to the guy's house and found the gas truck in the driveway, the owner's car and Bub's car parked behind it. The house had blown."

Vicki let out a huge sigh. "So all three of them were killed?"

"No. It looks like the gas company guy disappeared. Because the house didn't blow until Bub and his friend got there. The cops figure the gas guy disappeared when everyone else did, before he could fix the leak. Those guys coming inside in the morning to check on him must have sparked something that ignited the gas."

Vicki didn't know what to say. "I hate this," she said finally. "It's like we have to talk to everyone right away because you never know what's going to happen to them."

"Had your brother tried to tell him?"

"Yes."

"You never know, Vicki," Deacon said. "Something may have gotten through to him, even after you talked to him."

Vicki couldn't imagine, but she could hope. She thanked Deacon and said she hoped to run into him again sometime. She moved to the couch in the living room and sat crying softly. In a few minutes, Judd came looking for her.

She told him what had happened. "You see why school is going to be such a waste of time?" she said.

He shook his head. "I know it seems that way, but more kids might listen to us there than anywhere else."

"But will we be allowed to say anything? I wonder what everybody else makes of the disappearances and Carpathia and all that."

"I wonder, who'll be there and who won't," Judd said. "How many teachers and coaches and office people were raptured, and how many students?"

Late that afternoon, as Judd surfed the Internet, he realized how dramatically his life had changed in just a couple of weeks. He used to look for reasons to do anything but study or read. Now he had become a newshound, an information freak. He read his Bible, studied his notes from Bruce's sermons and private messages. Now he was searching the Net for anything else he could find about what was going on.

He heard a ping and saw the mail icon appear at the lower right side of his screen. Judd clicked on it and found a message from Bruce. "Judd, I will tell you and perhaps Vicki things I would not feel comfortable sharing with Lionel and Ryan. It isn't that I don't trust them, but these would be highly confidential matters, potentially dangerous if spread around. The younger boys might not know how to keep secrets or understand how important that is.

"Two members of the Tribulation Force, Captain Steele and Buck Williams (whom you know), run in some very interesting circles and may be able to shed light on international matters that others wouldn't be exposed to. I won't be able to tell you everything, but when I do, I'll count on your confidence—you know what that means: total secrecy. OK?"

Judd felt special that Bruce would trust him like that. When he answered, he would assure Bruce he could be trusted. Meanwhile, Bruce told him the story of Buck Williams having met Israel's Chaim Rosenzweig, the botanist who had created a formula that allowed desert sands to bloom like a greenhouse. The result had made Israel one of the richest nations in the world. Buck Williams had interviewed him and become his friend after Rosenzweig had been named *Global Weekly's* Man of the Year. Rosenzweig had introduced Buck to Nicolae Carpathia.

"I've been most encouraged by your attitude, your intelligence, and your curiosity, Judd," Bruce wrote. "You might be interested in the text of an interview with Dr. Rosenzweig. You will find it at the following Web site."

Judd quickly clicked on it. Bruce was right. Judd found it fascinating.

Wallace Theodore of ABC TV's *Nightline* had interviewed Rosenzweig, and the text had been stored on the site. Judd found the following most intriguing and looked forward to when he might talk with Buck Williams personally about it.

WT: Dr. Rosenzweig, what can you tell us about Nicolae Carpathia?

CR: I found him most impressive. So bright, so engaging, so articulate, so humble—

WT: Excuse, me, sir. Humble?

CR: Probably as humble as any leader I have ever met. Never have I seen a man like this.

When he was invited to speak at the United Nations not a month ago, he almost declined, he felt so unworthy. But you heard the speech. I would have nominated him for Prime Minister of Israel, if he were eligible!

Mr. Theodore, he has ideas upon ideas! He speaks so many languages that he hardly ever needs an interpreter, even for some of the remotest tribes.

WT: How can Carpathia give away *your* formula?

NC: I was more than happy to offer it. Botswana will soon be one of the most fertile countries in all of Africa, if not the world.

WT: Having the formula made Israel a wealthy nation. Russia attacked you for the formula alone.

CR: It's not about money, Mr. Theodore. I need none. Israel needs none.

WT: Then what could Carpathia offer that is worthy of trade?

CR: What has Israel prayed for since the beginning of time as the chosen people of God? *Shalom.* Peace. 'Pray for the peace of Israel.'

WT: Many say God supernaturally protected you against the Russian attack. With God on your side, do you need to barter with Nicolae Carpathia for protection?

CR: We pray, we seek God, but in the meantime we believe he helps those who help themselves.

WT: And you're helping yourselves by . . . ?

CR: The formula is tied to Carpathia's disarmament policy. Once the world is disarmed, Israel should not have to worry about her borders. Any nation threatening Israel will suffer immediate extinction, using the weaponry available to the UN, 10 percent from each donating country. Imagine the firepower.

WT: But Carpathia doesn't believe in war.

CR: He also knows that the best way to keep the peace is to have the weapons to enforce it.

WT: And how long does this agreement between Israel and Carpathia last?

CR: Mr. Carpathia suggested that full rights to the formula would return to us after only seven years.

Judd froze. So there it was, the seven-year agreement between Israel and the Antichrist. Judd called Bruce at the church office. "Does this say what I think it says?"

"It sure does," Bruce said. "How many will recognize it for what it is, I can't say. But here's another tidbit for you, and please tell no one other than Vicki, and swear her to secrecy as well: Buck Williams has been invited to Israel for the signing of the treaty."

Judd shook his head. "Can you get him to tell us about it when he gets back?"

"No promises. He may have to lie low and not be seen with believers for a while. But if he can and we find a way to make it happen, I'll do my best."

On Monday a week later, Vicki awoke at the crack of dawn. Her schoolbooks had burned with her trailer, she barely remembered her class schedule, and she dreaded the thought of going back. She would miss Clarice Washington, Lionel's older sister, with whom she had sat on the school bus. Clarice had been raptured, and Vicki would not ride the bus anyway; she would ride with Judd. He would drop Lionel and Ryan off at Global Community Junior High on the way. What a joke.

She knew the first day back to high school would be chaotic when she saw what was happening at the junior high.

SEVEN

Back to School

JUDD felt queasy when he joined the heavy traffic wending its way to the junior high school. Lionel had fallen strangely silent since the four kids got into the car, but Ryan had kept up a steady stream of chatter. The only thing Vicki had said was that she wondered if anyone would recognize her. Judd did not recall noticing her in the past, but there was a vast difference between the hard-looking, black-lipped, and black-eyelidded girl he had met and this preppy version that sat beside him now.

For many of the junior highers, this merely looked like the first day of school again. Everyone seemed carefully dressed and equipped, and their mothers or fathers dropped them off, watching anxiously as they headed inside.

"Wonder how many kids lost parents,"

Ryan said. "Man, have I got something for show-and-tell."

"They still do show-and-tell?" Vicki asked.

"No, but for sure everybody's gonna want to be telling where they were and what they saw and who they know who's gone and all that."

Judd glanced in the rearview mirror and noticed Lionel nodding, but he was gazing out the window. Judd spoke softly to Vicki. "You gonna go to the office and see about getting new books?"

"I guess," she said. "They'll probably charge me."

"If you need any mon—"

"I know, Judd," she said quickly. "Thanks. I'll let you know. But I'm going to find a job soon."

"You don't have to do that."

"Oh, yes I do. I'm not a freeloader or a charity case."

"Let me get out here!" Ryan said. "I see some of the guys!"

"Just wait," Judd said. "We've got to talk about what you're going to say about your situation."

"My situation? What do you mean? My parents are dead. How else can I say it? You think I'm going to start crying or something? I don't think I can cry anymore."

Judd pulled into the line circling the entrance, and they crawled along. "Both you and Lionel have to come up with some story about where you're staying."

"You mean lie?"

"'Course not. But you don't have to tell people you're living with other kids. Just say you're staying with someone from church."

"Good idea," Lionel said. "I'm not sure I'm ready to tell everybody that I'm the only one left in my family. But I'll bet they try to get us talking about what we think happened. If they ask me, I'll tell 'em."

Judd pulled over and shifted into Park. "You guys are sure you want to walk all the way home after school?"

"It's not that far," Lionel said. "Anyway, it's either wait here for you for an hour or go home. Nothing else to do."

Judd nodded. Vicki said, "We're going to want to hear all about it, so try to remember everything."

"All right, all right," Ryan said. "Let's go already! Unlock the doors."

"They might ask kids whose parents are gone to fill out new emergency forms," Judd said.

"And we'll put down Bruce Barnes's name and the church's phone number," Ryan said. "We've been through this a gazillion times."

Judd unlocked the doors, and it seemed Lionel was out as quickly as Ryan. "All of a sudden I feel like a parent," Judd said, pulling back into traffic. "I could've waited ten years to start worrying about what a couple of junior highers are going to do all day."

Vicki just smiled and nodded. She looked tense.

In the parking lot at the former Prospect High School, teachers and coaches and office staff directed traffic and spoke through bullhorns. "Don't worry about parking stickers today! We'll deal with that later! Check the bulletin boards for class and schedule changes! We'll be on a shortened program today, starting in the field house for an all-school assembly! Sit with your class!"

"Homeroom?" Judd asked through the window.

"No, your whole class. Freshmen in the west balcony, sophomores in the east balcony, juniors in the back on the main floor, seniors in front."

Vicki appeared pale and on the verge of tears as she got out of the car. "You want to stay with me for that opening assembly?" Judd said.

She sighed. "I really would. You think they'd let me?"

"You don't look like a freshman anyway,"

he said. "You may have to join your class if they go together, but otherwise, what are they going to do, kick you out?"

Judd waited as she stopped to ask a teacher what she should do about her books. "If that's all you lost, girl," the teacher said, "consider yourself lucky. We'll deal with that at the assembly. Don't be late."

The halls were as crowded as ever until they got into the field house. When the opening bell rang it was clear that the place, usually jammed for an all-school assembly, was only 70 to 75 percent filled. The teaching staff was depleted by about the same percentage, made obvious because they were sitting in rows on the platform behind the lectern.

As Judd and Vicki sat with the juniors, the principal, Mrs. Laverne Jenness, stepped to the microphone. "Welcome back," she said. "I'm proud to announce, in case you were under a rock and missed the news or the brand-spanking-new sign out front, that you are no longer Prospect Knights. You are Nicolae Carpathia Doves!"

She may have expected an enthusiastic response, because she appeared taken aback at a smattering of boos and laughter. But when the teachers jumped to their feet in applause, most of the students began cheering too. Judd thought at first that they were just mocking the teachers—as usual—but it soon became clear the celebrants were serious.

Mrs. Jenness beamed. "I'm so pleased that you're pleased," she said. "We recognize that this decision was made without your input, but there was nearly unanimous support at the administrative level. Really, your response is most gratifying. There had long been talk that our school name, steeped in history as it was, was unimaginative, merely echoing the name of the town in which we reside. And a knight is, of course, a warrior, which has long been an offensive mascot.

"To be named after so great and humble a leader and pacifist like UN Secretary-General Nicolae Carpathia, well, that should make us all proud."

The students chanted, "Nicolae High! Nicolae High! Nicolae High!"

Mrs. Jenness smiled, then raised her hands for silence. "I recognize that we reconvene only weeks after the most tragic event to ever curse our planet. Many of you lost friends and loved ones and will be grieving. Thank you for recognizing the importance of returning for your education, regardless. As you can imagine, the counseling services offered by our school district have been taxed beyond their limits. But as you see a need for a professional to talk to, please put your name on the waiting list. Don't be ashamed or afraid to ask. We're all trying to get through this."

Judd felt a nudge, and Vicki nodded toward a couple of seniors several rows ahead. "Are those Bibles?" she said.

"Looks like it," Judd said. "You know them?"

Vicki shook her head. "Hey, look."

A football coach Judd recognized approached the seniors and knelt in the aisle. He spoke earnestly to them, smiling, but came away with both Bibles. As he hurried past, Judd reached out and whispered, "What was that all about, Coach Handlesman?"

"Mind your own business, Thompson," Handlesman said. "We haven't allowed Bibles here since before you were born."

"But even now, after what happened?"

"Especially now," the coach said, moving on.

"Remember what they look like, Vicki," Judd said. "We're going to need all the friends we can get."

Mrs. Jenness droned on about the difficulties and trauma, the mixed classes, the complicated inconveniences. "Bear with us as we try to regroup and reschedule. The ratio of missing students and faculty seems fairly even, so class size should remain approximately the same as before.

"Those of you who lost textbooks, deal with that in each class and make your purchases in the bookstore by Friday. Now before I dismiss you, I would like to ask for your help. After an international tragedy that has struck so close to home, it's only natural to want to talk about it. It's therapeutic, and our counselors have advised me to let you have at it. Today in your abbreviated classes, we have asked faculty to get the housekeeping announcements out of the way, the book business taken care of, and any outlining of new class expectations dealt with quickly. Then they are free to supervise group discussions. Some of you will need to tell your stories of loss and fear. Others may choose not to speak of their ordeals. Please be respectful of those students and don't badger them for details before they're ready to be forthcoming.

"Now, here's what you can do for me. As you know, there has been widespread speculation about the cause of the vanishings. According to our consultants, part of the healing process—the making sense of this— involves forming and expressing your opinions on this. But I must remind you of the strict rule of the separation of church and state that has helped make this country great. We are a public institution, and this is not a forum in which we should espouse religious views.

"I am aware that one of the many explanations for what happened is religious in nature. I'm not saying it has no validity. Like most of you, I lost extended family members. Their closest relatives reminded me that those who disappeared predicted this and told us exactly what to make of such an occurrence.

"Though this happened among my own kin, and while those stories may even bear some scrutiny, I will not discuss them on school property during school hours. I'm asking that you not either. Even if I believed with all my heart that this was the best explanation for the disappearances—which, you may rest assured, I emphatically do not—I would maintain that this is the wrong venue in which to propagate that view. Thank you for understanding. I urge you to hold your questions until class time, unless anyone has something pressing that is appropriate to ask in front of the corporate body.

"All right, then. Oh, yes, son. A question from a junior boy. Please stand and state your name and your question loudly enough for me to hear and repeat it into the microphone. And if it is not something that pertains to the whole school, I would ask—"

"It pertains, ma'am!" Judd called out, rising, his heart thundering. "Judd Thompson, and I was just wondering if you would clarify this then!"

"Clarify which part, Mr. Thompson? What is unclear?"

"Why freedom of speech is extended only to those who hold certain views of what has happened?"

"This is not a freedom-of-speech issue, young man. It's a church-and-state issue. Thank you for raising it, but please don't make something of it that it is not. Dismissed!"

Judd was short of breath and knew his face was red as he gathered up his stuff. "I can't believe you did that," Vicki said, and he looked close to see if she was embarrassed or seemed to disapprove.

"That wasn't me," he said, shaking his head. "That was my evil twin. I've never done anything like that before in my life. I don't think I ever even paid attention in an assembly before."

"Hey, Judd, way to go, man," one of his classmates said, punching him on the shoulder. "Way to be raucous!"

Judd wanted to tell the boy he had been serious, but the guy was lost in the crowd. Coach Handlesman shouldered his way through to Judd and Vicki. "I liked you better when you made trouble by being a no-account, Thompson. Now you're angling to be a smart aleck, eh?"

"Nah. I just don't think there should be restrictions on people trying to figure out the truth."

"Cry me a river," the coach said, disappearing in the crowd.

"Be careful," Vicki said as they prepared to split up. "We don't want to be *too* conspicuous."

"What's your first class?" Judd said.

"Phys ed," she said. "Yours?"

"Psych."

"Should be interesting," she said.

Judd nodded but noticed Vicki was distracted. She was looking past him, and her face paled. "Shelly?" she said. "Shelly! Is that you?"

Judd had wanted to tell Vicki he would be praying for her, but that sounded cheesy, and she was preoccupied anyway. And his psych class with Mr. Shellenberger was at the complete other end of the school.

EIGHT

Opposition

VICKI had not intended to ignore Judd or abandon him, but he was gone before she knew it. She had not seen or heard from her former neighbor Shelly since the day they both discovered what had happened. To Vicki's horror, Shelly looked the same as she had that day. She stared into the distance as if she had seen things unspeakable.

"Are you all right, Shel?" Vicki asked.

Shelly looked at her, flat brown hair straight and lifeless, her pale green eyes vacant. "I don't know you," she said.

"Sure you do, Shelly. It's me, Vicki."

Shelly furrowed her brow and squinted. "No way," she said. "Vick, what happened to you?"

"To me?" It was out before Vicki could rein it in. Shelly was the one who didn't look like herself. Vicki may have been made up differently and dressed differently, but Shelly looked as if someone had punched her in the stomach.

"It's really you, Vicki?"

Vicki nodded. "Shelly, I know what happened. I lost my whole family, and—"

"I don't want to talk about it, OK? I really don't."

"But as awful as it was, Shelly, I—"

"Don't," she said, trembling.

"Leave her alone," an older girl said, glaring at Vicki. "Don't you know what happened to her?"

"No! What happened?"

"Don't tell her, Joyce!" Shelly said.

"You just get to class, Shelly. And don't let anybody make you say anything you don't want to say."

Shelly looked apologetically at Vicki and moved away. Joyce turned on Vicki. "Are you Byrne?"

"Yes, Joyce. Just dressing a little different these days."

"I'll say. Your trailer burned, right?"

Vicki nodded.

"So where you livin'?"

"Mount Prospect, with people from my church."

"That explains the threads. They makin' you dress that way?"

Vicki shook her head.

"So you didn't hear Shelly's story 'cause you haven't been back to the park?"

"Right."

"She was baby-sitting for the Fischers. You knew them."

Vicki nodded, moving toward the girls' locker room.

"One of the kids starts crying just when the parents get home. Shelly goes in to check on her, and the kid's really wailing. She picks her up, and that gets the little guy crying, so she picks him up too. Now she's got two squalling kids in her arms as the Fischers come in the door. She's about to explain that they just then woke up when both kids disappear and the parents too. Mom and Dad, poof, clothes in a pile right where they stood. The babies, gone with their pj's draped over Shelly's arms.

"Tell you the truth, it would have scared me to death, Vicki, but I wish I'd have seen it. Well, you know Shelly. She can't let it go. She's playing it over and over in her mind. I saw her the next afternoon, wandering through the trailer park, not saying a word to anybody."

"I saw her late that morning," Vicki said. "Same thing."

"I finally got her to tell me. Now everybody knows and nobody talks to her, figuring she doesn't want to talk about it. Which is true. But I think she feels like it was her fault somehow."

"Where you headed, Joyce?"

"Health. Next door here."

"You know what happened, don't you?"

"The disappearances? Sure. Jesus came back. What else? It's not like we haven't heard that all our lives."

"You believe that?"

"Sure, don't you?"

"Well, yeah," Vicki said, "but I didn't know you did."

"Don't worry, I'm not gonna get saved or anything. But look who went and who was left. Your mom and dad, right? And your little sister. But you were left. So was I. My whole family. How about Eddie? Bet your brother's still around."

"Gone," Vicki said.

"No kiddin'? Disappeared?"

Vicki nodded.

"That might prove me wrong. He was no Holy Joe, was he?"

"He became a believer after he got to Mich—"

"See? I knew it! What else could it be, Vick? Huh?"

"But that doesn't make you want to be a Christian?"

"No way! I still think the whole thing sounds wacky."

"Even though you believe it's true?"

"*Especially* because I believe it's true. Hey, I *know* it's true. If that was God's idea of how to do things, I want no part of it. How about you?"

"I believe it too. And I plan to be included when Jesus comes back again."

"Well, good for you, girl. You're not going to set your sights on me, are ya?"

"Well, I wish you would—"

"Oh, you are, aren't you? I'm going to be a project, just like my mom was to Mrs. Fischer. Save your breath. I don't need any convincing. I believe, and I've chosen. So turn those Bible guns on somebody else. Like Shelly. She'd be perfect. Gotta go."

Psychology was one class Judd had actually enjoyed, and Mr. Shellenberger was the reason. He was a tall, fleshy man with a generous nose and receding, wavy hair. He had a sonorous voice, a superior manner, and he loved to bestow his opinions on one and all. He was in rare form today.

"OK, class," he began, "listen up. Parking-lot stickers in the office, new books in the bookstore—title, if you forgot already, is on the board. Now let's do some practical psychology. Let's vent our traumas and deepest fears for the benefit and enjoyment of all. I'll start."

The class chuckled.

"First, is there anyone in here who will turn me into the thought police if I discuss the religious theory? Anyone? No one? Don't be intimidated. If you're going to gum up the school year with an expensive lawsuit, tell me now, and I'll avoid the subject. Speak now or forever hold your peace. Very well, the God thing:

"Jesus didn't come to get the good people and leave the bad. There are some who actually believe that, you know. Anyone here want to stake claim to that view? Nothing to be ashamed of. Some very respected people have fessed up to it. Come on. Anyone? No one? Mr. Thompson! Really? I thought you acted the agitator this morning just to get a rise out of our fearless leader. That was out of character for you, though. Well, isn't this just too interesting? Do you care to discuss it?"

Judd shrugged. He was no match for an intellect, a presence, like Mr. Shellenberger. Judd had considered hiding his belief, but he wouldn't have been able to live with that much cowardice.

"I've already stated my opinion," the teacher said, "so I promise not to try to shred your belief system. Tell me, is this new for you? Apparently it is, because if you had held this belief before, and your theory is right, you'd have been taken by Jesus too, right?"

Judd nodded.

"So, who convinced you? Let me guess. A parent."

"In a way."

"Hmm. One that was left or one that was taken?"

"Both were taken."

Mr. Shellenberger suddenly grew serious, his face grave. His volume fell, and he appeared truly different. "Mr. Thompson, forgive me if I have offended you. I meant to ask at the beginning how many of you lost immediate family members in the vanishings. Let me back up and do that."

Half a dozen of the thirty kids raised their hands.

"How many lost extended family?"

Eight or ten more raised their hands.

"How many of you lost people you knew well or cared about?"

Another half dozen or so.

"And how many of you feel almost isolated from this, having lost virtually no one in your orbit?"

Four kids raised their hands.

"Now then," the teacher continued, his tone still subdued, "regardless of my personal view of this—which you may be assured I will impart—I do not take lightly the losses. Mr. Thompson, I am sorry for your losses. Did you lose other family members?"

"My brother and sister, twins."

Mr. Shellenberger stood towering over the students, his arms folded, a hand under his chin. "Mm-hm," he said. "Religious family?"

Religious was not a word Judd's family used. But he knew what the teacher was driving at. He nodded.

"And you were the only one left behind."

"Right," Judd said.

"It is not surprising at all that you find comfort in ascribing these losses to something divine. It has to make you feel better to believe your family is in heaven with God."

"Somewhat."

"I wouldn't denigrate that. You will outgrow it, but I'm sure it's of great benefit to you now. It may be years before you will be able to differentiate the very real confidence you feel from the defense mechanism your mind has provided."

"So I believe because I have to?"

"Excellent. Exactly. Don't get me wrong. Right now this is as real to you as if it were literally true. Our perceptions, as I have said many times, are our realities. If you perceive I despise you and you will never succeed in this class, that is reality to you. If you believe the opposite, regardless of what you know about me, the opposite will be real for you."

Judd wondered why he had never detected the silliness of the man's logic before.

"Let me ask you, Mr. Thompson, what you now believe is the reason that your family was taken and you were not?"

"I was never really a believer. They were."

"Really? Where did you fall short?"

"I just told you. I didn't buy into it. I knew what was being taught. When I was younger I was more devout."

"But not devout enough?"

"I never actually made the commitment to Christ."

"Mm-hm. Class, anyone? We're not arguing here, and I would be loath to try to talk Mr. Thompson out of a belief that has to be therapeutic for him, but someone tell me what he's really feeling now."

"Survivor's remorse," came a low voice from the back. "Just like soldiers who come back from war."

"Very good," Mr. Shellenberger said. "I'm not asking you to concede the point today or even this year, Mr. Thompson. But file it away. Let it work on you a little. You feel like the unworthy one, and yet you are the lone survivor."

"That's why I was the survivor! I *was* the unworthy one."

"You're asking, 'Why me?'"

"I know why."

"OK, very interesting. Someone else?"

A girl raised her hand. "You were going to tell us your opinion. You've said what it was not, so what was it?"

"Well, it was *not* a lot of things. I don't believe it was space aliens. I don't believe an enemy could be so surgical, taking certain ones and leaving others. No doubt it was something cosmic, perhaps even psychic or metaphysical. But the result was physical. I lean toward the hypothesis of Nicolae Carpathia and Dr. Chaim Rosenzweig of Israel, who ascribe the phenomenon to some nuclear reaction. We have stockpiled so many nuclear weapons that it was only a matter of time before something in the atmosphere—electricity, energy, magnetism, something—triggered a reaction.

"I should say this, however. Admittedly mine is a personal observation and far from scientific. But it seems to me that those who were taken, generally and on the whole, mind you, were of a slightly lower intellect than those who were left. I come from an extremely intelligent and highly educated extended family. We lost no blood relatives. I did lose colleagues I respected and admired, but in fairness, I have to say they were not quite the academic equals of those left behind. I have no idea what that means."

You sure don't, Judd thought.

NINE

Vicki's Battle

VICKI'S first-period class met in the gym normally used for volleyball practice. The girls sat on the floor and got the standard announcements about books, parking permits, and even gym clothes. Then her P.E. teacher sat on the floor and gathered the class around her. Mrs. Waltonen, in her midforties, was thin and dark with short hair and glasses.

"What do you make of all the children disappearing?" she said. "That's the part I can't figure out."

"You can figure out the rest?" someone said.

"Well, no. But if this is what a lot of people think it is, why would all the babies, even unborn babies, and toddlers and little kids be taken?"

"What do most people think it is?" a girl asked.

"You know," Mrs. Waltonen said. "The subject we aren't supposed to raise."

"Most people think it's that?" a tiny girl next to Vicki said. "I thought that was just a few of the crazies. I don't think that, and nobody I know does."

"We're not supposed to discuss it, at any rate," Mrs. Waltonen said. "Let's just express some feelings."

"I have a question," Vicki said, raising her hand.

Mrs. Waltonen squinted at her, and Vicki knew the woman was wondering who she was.

"Vicki Byrne," Vicki said. "Um—"

"Without all the makeup," the teacher said. "I like the look."

Vicki blushed. "Thanks."

"Your makeup disappear?" someone said, and several laughed.

"What's your question, Vicki?"

"If you think most people think what happened was what you said, why can't we talk about it?"

Mrs. Waltonen shook her head and sighed. "You heard what I heard. I don't know. Seems nothing should be off-limits now. We have the freedom to talk about everything else under the sun, including stuff I never thought I'd hear in public, but not God. No way."

"Then don't!" someone called out. "If I hear another person say they think Jesus did this, I'm gonna croak!"

"All right," Mrs. Waltonen said. "Let's move on." She asked for a show of hands for those who had lost family members and so on.

Someone asked, "Did you lose anyone?"

Mrs. Waltonen pressed her lips together. "I'm, ah, trying to get through this right now," she said, her voice quavering. "We lost a grandchild."

To Vicki it seemed the groan of pain and sympathy came from the whole class.

"How old?"

"A baby. Not six months."

"That's awful."

"We miss her terribly. Her father, my son-in-law, also disappeared. And we lost my husband's sister and her whole family, her husband and three kids."

"No way God did that," a girl said.

Several others nodded and grunted in agreement. Vicki wanted to scream. Instead, she asked, "Anything different about your sister-in-law and her family? Any clues why them?"

"Well, see, I can't talk about that without getting in trouble."

"Talk about it!" a girl hollered. "We won't tell."

"No!" someone else said. "We're not supposed to, so let's not!"

Vicki turned to see who had said that, and while she couldn't tell, from the looks on the faces behind her, it could have been anyone. They were angry. In the back she saw a few confused, sorrowful faces.

Wasn't this just a little too obvious? The one explanation that made sense, that most people were aware of, that many had been warned about, was the one they were not allowed to discuss. And why? Because of the separation of church and state? Vicki suddenly felt very old.

Like Judd, she found herself bolder than she had ever been. She had been so lazy and lackadaisical in gym class that she usually skipped it or sat out, making up a litany of complaints, illnesses, and injuries. She had never responded to Mrs. Waltonen or to any other teachers. It just hadn't been her style.

Now Vicki felt like an agitator. A rebel for another cause. She had been against the status quo before. But now she was *for* something. "If we're not going to talk about what obviously is the truth about what happened," she said, "let's hear some other explanation."

That started it. Angry words were tossed about, several girls raising their voices. "You believe it was God?" several said. "Where've you been? And why are you still here?"

Finally Mrs. Waltonen calmed them. "Vicki is right," she said. "Let's hear what others think happened."

Silence.

"Surely someone has an opinion."

A soft-spoken girl in the back said, "Who could ever know? I mean, really. Certain people disappeared; others didn't. Some in the same family. Almost as many women and men, but all babies and young children. I know a twelve-year-old who is still here, and a friend of mine said she knows a ten-year-old, but I don't know. These kids' mothers are wailing all over the place. This is like the worst horror movie you could ever see."

"Yeah, but we're *in* this one."

"Yeah."

"Personally," a girl sitting by herself said, "I think it was some big science experiment that went bad."

"That could be."

"Yeah, I never thought of that."

"Right, like a scientist figured out how to beam stuff like in the old *Star Trek* movies, only he beamed the wrong people and can't bring them back."

"I think they're coming back," one said.

"You do? Why?"

"I have to. I'd go nuts otherwise. If I lost somebody in a wreck or I knew they died of some disease, that would be one thing. But these people didn't die. At least I hope they didn't."

"Some people died."

"Not the ones who disappeared. Just people who, like, got run over because of someone else disappearing."

"You don't know the ones who disappeared are still alive."

"I do," Vicki said.

"You can't know that!"

"Fine, but I do."

"You might believe it, Vicki, but you can't know."

"Then why do I know?"

"You don't. You just think you know."

"If my granddaughter is alive," Mrs. Waltonen said, "I'd like to know that. I agree you can't really know, Vicki. But tell me why you think so, and tell me where you think she is."

Vicki looked around. It seemed people were actually curious. "But isn't somebody going to get me in trouble with the church/

state police? I guess my freedom of speech goes only so far."

"So you think Mrs. Waltonen's baby is in heaven with Jesus."

"I know she is."

"You can't know that! And if you did, you'd be there too!"

"If I had known in advance, I would be, yes. With my parents and my brother and sister."

"Whoop, there it is!" a girl cried out. "You lost your family, so you've got to come up with some nice explanation. That's all right. You're entitled. No offense to Mrs. Waltonen, but you two can believe whatever you want so you feel better about who you lost. That's all. I'd like to know where the girls are who aren't here today. What about that fat girl who was such a good athlete? And those twins nobody could stand? And that girl with the bad face and the—"

"All right," Mrs. Waltonen said, "I think that's enough detail. I have a list here of the girls in the class who are known to have disappeared in the vanishings. The ones you mentioned are included, yes. Mary Alice—you know her? She's out sick today. And Francis also disappeared. There are two others, Barb and Sue, who are assumed to have disappeared."

The girls sat silently for a moment, a few weeping. Finally someone said, "Do you hear how this sounds? We're sitting here talking about people we knew disappearing."

And no one, Vicki thought, *seems to want to face the truth*. As wild as the truth seemed, it sure made more sense than the crazy ideas she'd heard.

"Is there anybody else who believes this was the rapture of the church?" Vicki blurted, and she scanned the group.

It seemed everyone responded at once, waving her off, groaning, saying no. But she saw the look of hope on the teacher's face, and a couple of girls at the edge of the group just looked sadly at her.

"Stop talking about it!" came a voice over the din. "We were told not to, so don't! You're pushing your personal religious beliefs on us, and that's wrong!"

Vicki was mad. "I don't accuse you of forcing your beliefs on me when you tell me it was aliens or *Star Trek* scientists. Don't you have a brain? Can't you think for yourself? Do you need to hide behind some rule about the separation of church and state, so you don't hear something that might mess up your mind?"

"Vicki!" Mrs. Waltonen said. "That's enough."

"Can I ask about the separation thing then?" Vicki said.

"It depends."

"It's just a question about the history of it. Where did it come from?"

"I've heard different theories," Mrs. Waltonen said. "I know it's not in the Constitution, but I believe it came from those who wanted to protect citizens from having their religious freedom threatened by the government. One of our freedoms is the right to believe and to worship without the government telling us what church we have to belong to."

"That's what I thought," Vicki said, knowing she had heard something about this, maybe from her dad, whom she had ignored. "So when did it get turned around to protect the government from religion?"

"I'm sorry?"

"You said the separation of church and state was designed to keep the government out of the church. Now it's used to keep the church out of the government."

Mrs. Waltonen raised her eyebrows, but several girls said things like, "That's the way it should be!"

"Even if it was a law, which it's not," Vicki said, "it would be no good if it violated the right to free speech. I have the freedom to say whatever I want, except here."

"Good!"

"Yeah, shut up!"

"Let her talk!"

"She's talked enough! And when did she start talking anyway? I don't even remember her from this class!"

"You do too! That's Vicki Byrne!"

"Well, when did she start caring about anything?"

"What's happening to us?" someone said, tears in her voice. "I thought we were supposed to discuss this to start coming to some closure."

"Closure? You sound like a talk-show host! How are we going to have closure on something like this?"

"That's right," Vicki said, "especially when certain theories are out of bounds?"

The bell rang, and the gym quickly emptied, but Vicki noticed that Mrs. Waltonen was gazing at her. When Vicki returned the glance, the teacher said nothing but did not look away. Vicki felt as if Mrs. Waltonen was trying to communicate something to her—exactly what, she did not know. The quiet girls in the back were also some of the last to leave, and they peeked at her too.

Was there something here, some core of a

group that might agree with her or at least be willing to listen? Vicki decided to spend the rest of the day bringing these issues up in every class. Maybe she wouldn't be as aggressive as she had been in gym class, but she would say enough to get people arguing about freedom of speech and whether God had anything to do with the disappearances. Somehow she would get an inkling of how many believers or potential believers there were at this school.

Vicki didn't want one more person to die before she at least had the chance to tell them what she believed.

TEN

The Big Idea

On the way to his last class before lunch, Judd saw the two senior boys whose Bibles had been confiscated during the assembly. One was tall and blond, the other stockier and dark-haired. He didn't know their names, but if his memory was right, they were smart kids—science club, honor roll types. "Hey," he said, approaching them, "are you believers?"

They looked wary. "Why? Are you?"

He had to take the chance. "I am."

"How do we know you're not playing us, trying to get us in trouble?" the blond said.

"You don't."

"Well," Dark Hair said, "how did you become a believer?"

"Lost my family," Judd said. "I knew the truth all along."

"Then you should know what Christians are called during this period."

"You mean tribulation saints?"

The two looked at each other and smiled. They extended their hands. "John," the blond said.

"Mark," the other said.

"You're kidding, right?" Judd said. "John and Mark?"

"We're cousins."

"But I mean—"

"We know what you mean. Yeah, we were named after the disciples. Churchgoers all our lives. We lost everybody in our family except one aunt. We're living with her and going to a church in Arlington Heights. What's your story?"

Judd ran it down quickly. Then, "Gotta go, but let's talk again. We should get our church groups together sometime."

"That's for sure," John said. "Especially if they're not going to even let us carry our Bibles to school. Coach Handlesman said we might not even get them back."

"What? You're kidding!"

They shook their heads.

"Are we going to be in a police state or what?" Judd said.

"It's like martial law," Mark said.

Judd waved as he headed toward Current History. "See ya tomorrow."

"Yeah," John called after him, "if we're still free men."

"Not funny, John!" came the gruff voice of Coach Handlesman.

Judd began to wonder if he and Vicki, and even John and Mark, should be more covert and lie low. It was one thing to be a bold witness, but if they got kicked out or were known as dangerous people to be seen with, what good would they be?

His history teacher, an old spinster named Miss June, looked as if she had been through a war. Normally tidy and fastidious, today she looked disheveled. Her shoes were scuffed, her blouse wrinkled, her hair pinned in place without much thought. Her fingers trembled, and she sat behind her desk rather than standing as usual.

"Well, class, I have been through some things in my day, but I never would have dreamed that hearing everyone's stories would have been nearly as traumatic as experiencing this tragedy one's self. I'm wondering if you might agree that we have had enough talk on this subject by now, and perhaps we can talk about the rest of the quarter."

No one said anything.

"All right then?" she said.

"Um, no," a boy said from the back row. "What's to talk about? You're going to streamline the course because of the time we missed, and we'll start getting assignments tomorrow. What else is there?"

"We could talk about what we're going to be studying," she said.

"We already know that. Current History is current history. Let's talk about who's not coming back to this class."

Miss June pursed her lips and gave the boy a disgusted look. She studied her attendance printout, but when she began announcing the names of seven students who were either confirmed disappeared (four), whereabouts unknown (one), and ill (two), her voice broke. Soon she could not continue.

"What in the world is wrong, Miss June?" a girl said. "How many people did you lose?"

But she could not speak. She just pressed a hand to her mouth and shook her head.

"This I've got to hear," the boy behind Judd said, and Judd glared at him.

"Give her a break," he said. "If you didn't lose anybody, at least be sensitive to those of us who did."

The boy pantomimed as if playing a violin.

"Can we talk about it among ourselves?" a girl said. Miss June nodded. "Because I know it wasn't a religious thing."

"We're not supposed to talk about that!"

"Oh, who's going to stop us?" the girl said.

"Anyway, I'm saying it *wasn't* that. How can they have a problem with that?"

Judd's resolve to keep quiet disappeared. "You *know* it wasn't a religious thing?" he said.

"That's right," she said. "Not one person in my church disappeared. So what does that tell you?"

"That you don't believe in Jesus!" a husky guy in the back called out, and several laughed, including him.

"But we do!" she said. "We all do! We believe in all the sons of God."

"What does that mean?"

"We're not supposed to be—"

"Put a sock in it! I want to know what her church believes!"

"We believe that everybody's a son of God, like Jesus. Buddha, Confucius, Muhammad, Jesus, all the great moral leaders and great teachers."

Judd said, "So you believe Jesus is *a* son of God but not *the* Son of God."

"Not the only one, no. We're all children of God."

"So Jesus isn't God."

"Of course not, silly. God is God. There is only one God."

"So you don't believe the Bible."

"Of course we do. We accept all the sacred writings."

"Like what?"

"The Bible, the Torah, the Talmud, the—"

"And they all say that Jesus is God and is the only way to God?" Judd said.

"No! None of them say that! God is not the exclusive property of Christianity. There are many roads to God."

"The Bible says Jesus is God and that he's the only way to God."

"I don't believe that."

"That it's true or that the Bible says it?"

"Either one!"

"Then that's why you're still here."

"Oh!" someone shouted. "He burned you! But he's still here too, ain't he?"

"That's enough," Miss June said, rising and wiping her nose. "This is the very reason we're not to be getting into this aspect of it. Now if you're going to insist on discussing this, let's keep it nonsectarian."

"What does that mean?"

"Keep religion out of it, especially specific ones."

"Yeah," someone said, "like those ones where everyone was left behind!"

Miss June was weeping again. "I don't see any humor in this! Aren't you people the least bit scared? I'm terrified! I can make no sense of this, and there seems no recourse. If someone would come forward and take credit for it, make some demands, tell how he or she did it, we could get our minds around it. But this . . . this . . . crazy, unexplainable mystery! Every morning I wake up and pray it was a dream, that it will end, that it will all be made plain. Talk about it, kids. Talk about how it made you feel."

That served to silence the class. It was clear they didn't want to talk about it. Judd glanced around. The kids were somber again. No wisecracks. "It scared me to death," he said. "I was on an airplane when it happened."

The classroom was deathly still as Judd spoke. "The guy next to me disappeared while I was dozing. He was a big, heavy guy, and I couldn't figure out at first how he could have climbed over me without waking me. Then I saw his clothes there in a pile. Everybody else was discovering people missing at the same time. What a mess! I'm amazed there wasn't more panic. People thought their seatmates had gone to the bathroom, but too many were gone, and what was with all the piles of clothes and shoes and jewelry and glasses?"

Judd told how he had lost his whole immediate family, but he said nothing about how he knew what had happened. He just wanted to get kids talking, trying to find out who leaned his way and who might already be a believer. His own high school had already been named after the Antichrist, and he knew he and Vicki were going to need all the friends they could get.

At lunchtime Judd looked for Vicki. Juniors and freshmen shared the cafeteria, but he had not known her before and had no idea where she sat. He finally spotted her in a corner with a bunch of girls who looked the way Vicki described herself before the Rapture. They must have been friends from her trailer park.

Judd wanted to talk with her, but he didn't want to barge in either. He sat near their table and heard some of the conversation. The girls were telling Vicki they missed her and wondered what had happened to her. "I've been hammered every night since," one said. "How else do you cope with something like this?"

A heavyset girl sitting next to Vicki said, "Apparently you change your life and get preppy all of a sudden."

The others smiled. Vicki didn't. "I lost my whole family, you know," she said.

"You lost your mind too," the girl said. "Look at you."

Judd decided it was time to give Vicki an

out. He walked past her table so she could see him. If she didn't want to acknowledge him, that was all right too. Maybe she didn't want to confirm that she even ran with a crowd that looked like him. That would make her transformation too complete.

Vicki was thrilled to see Judd, and she jumped at the chance to escape. "Judd!" she said. "Can I sit with you? We need to talk."

"Sure."

"What'sa matter?" a girl said. "We're not good enough for you anymore?"

"I'm not good enough for you anymore," Vicki said. "Since I'm wearing borrowed clothes and they don't look like yours—"

"They look like somebody's mother's clothes," the big girl said, but Vicki didn't respond. She and Judd took their trays outside.

"There's a reason these look like someone's mother's clothes," she whispered.

He nodded. They brought each other up to date on their mornings. "This is going to be hard, isn't it?" he said.

"You're telling me. But, Judd, I just feel like this is where we're supposed to be, doing what we're meant to be doing."

"Out loud or in secret? Sounds like neither of us got very far by being open."

"I found a few people I think might be with us, and those two seniors—"

"John and Mark," Judd said.

"Yeah. We've got to stick together somehow."

"We need more people. We can't just be a secret, private club. We've got to do something."

"I've been thinking about that, Judd," Vicki said. "I think there's something we can do."

"That won't get us kicked out of Nicolae High?"

"If we do it right. Your computer is the latest thing, right?"

"There's not much it can't do."

"Including publishing?"

"Desktop publishing? 'Course. It was made for that."

Vicki started gathering up her stuff. "Walk with me," she said as she took her tray inside. "And let's talk to Lionel and Ryan about this when we get home."

"About what?"

"An underground newspaper. We'll have to think of a good title for it, but it will tell people's stories without giving away their identities. We can use lots of prophecy and stuff from Bruce, and we can just leave piles of them around where anyone can get them. They don't have to be long, but we have to keep them coming. If Bruce is right and we can put a few predictions in there that actually come true, kids will want these. Who knows how many kids might become believers?"

Judd slid his tray onto the retrieval rack and stood back, looking at Vicki. "Why didn't I think of that?" he said.

"You like the idea?"

"It's perfect!"

"That's another thing we need more of in the Young Trib Force," she said.

"What," he said, "more perfect ideas?"

"I was thinking of more women," she said. "Same thing."

ABOUT THE AUTHORS

Jerry B. Jenkins (www.jerryjenkins.com) is the author of more than one hundred books. The former vice president for publishing for the Moody Bible Institute of Chicago, he also served many years as editor of *Moody* magazine. His writing has appeared in a variety of publications, including *Reader's Digest, Parade,* in-flight magazines, and many Christian periodicals. He writes books in four genres: biographies, marriage and family, fiction for children, and fiction for adults.

Jenkins's biographies include books with Hank Aaron, Bill Gaither, Luis Palau, Walter Payton, Orel Hershiser, Nolan Ryan, Brett Butler, and Billy Graham, among many others. The Hershiser, Ryan, and Graham books reached the *New York Times* best-sellers list.

Five of his apocalyptic novels, coauthored with Tim LaHaye, *Left Behind, Tribulation Force, Nicolae, Soul Harvest,* and *Apollyon,* have appeared on the Christian Booksellers Association's best-selling fiction list and the *Publishers Weekly* religion best-sellers list. *Left Behind* was nominated for Novel of the Year by the Evangelical Christian Publishers Association in both 1997 and 1998.

As a marriage and family author and speaker, Jenkins has been a frequent guest on Dr. James Dobson's *Focus on the Family* radio program.

Jerry is also the writer of the nationally syndicated sports story comic strip *Gil Thorp,* distributed to newspapers across the United States by Tribune Media Services.

Jerry and Dianna and their sons live in northeastern Illinois and in Colorado.

Speaking engagement bookings available through speaking@jerryjenkins.com.

Dr. Tim LaHaye is a noted author, minister, counselor, television commentator, and nationally recognized speaker on family life and Bible prophecy. He is the founder and president of Family Life Seminars and the founder of The PreTrib Research Center. Presently Dr. LaHaye speaks at many of the major Bible prophecy conferences in the U.S. and Canada, where his seven current prophecy books are very popular.

Dr. LaHaye is a graduate of Bob Jones University and holds an M.A. and Doctor of Ministry degree from Western Conservative Theological Seminary. For twenty-five years he pastored one of the nation's outstanding churches in San Diego, which grew to three locations. It was during that time that he founded two accredited Christian high schools, a Christian school system of ten schools, and Christian Heritage College.

Dr. LaHaye has written over forty nonfiction books, with over eleven million copies in print in thirty-two languages. He has written books on a wide variety of subjects, such as family life, temperaments, and Bible prophecy. His current fiction works written with Jerry Jenkins, *Left Behind, Tribulation Force, Nicolae, Soul Harvest,* and *Apollyon* have all reached number one on the Christian best-seller charts. Other works by Dr. LaHaye are *Spirit-Controlled Temperament; How to Be Happy though Married; Revelation, Illustrated and Made Plain;* and the youth fiction series, *Left Behind: The Kids.*

He is the husband of Beverly LaHaye, founder of Concerned Women for America. Together they have four children and nine grandchildren. Snow skiing, waterskiing, motorcycling, golfing, vacationing with family, and jogging are among his leisure activities.

The Future Is Clear

In one shocking moment, millions around the globe disappear. Those left behind face an uncertain future—especially the four kids who now find themselves alone.

Best-selling authors Jerry B. Jenkins and Tim LaHaye present the Rapture and Tribulation through the eyes of four friends—Judd, Vicki, Lionel, and Ryan. As the world falls in around them, they band together to find faith and fight the evil forces that threaten their lives.

#1: The Vanishings Four friends face Earth's last days together.

#2: Second Chance The kids search for the truth.

#3: Through the Flames The kids risk their lives.

#4: Facing the Future The kids prepare for battle.

#5: Nicolae High The Young Trib Force goes back to school.

#6: The Underground The Young Trib Force fights back.

BOOKS #7 AND #8 COMING SOON!